The grass was too prickly and
the earth was too hard.
The trees were too noisy but
the desert was too quiet.

The sun was too hot but
the night was too cold.
His family were warm but
they wriggled too much.

Everybody knows that lions
need a lot of sleep, and
Arlo was EXHAUSTED.

"Will I ever sleep again?" Arlo sighed.
But Arlo wasn't the only one who was awake.

"Of course you will," said a voice from above.
"I sleep through the day when it's bright, noisy and hot.
Shall I tell you how?" And the owl began to sing . . .

"Have a good stretch from your nose to your toes.
Do a little wriggle, let your eyes gently close.

Relax your whole body, slow your breathing right down,
Imagine you're sinking into the soft ground.

Think about places where you'd like to be,
The things that you'd do there and what you might see.

As you fall into calmness, so comfy and deep,
Your mind will rest and you'll drift off to sleep."

Arlo stretched, wriggled and tried to relax,
while Owl sang her song once more.

Arlo thought of the places he would like to go and see. He imagined bounding up mountains, wading in rivers and climbing enormous trees.

Then Arlo imagined he might need a rest,
so he pictured himself cuddled up with his
cosy, snoring family. And before he knew it . . .

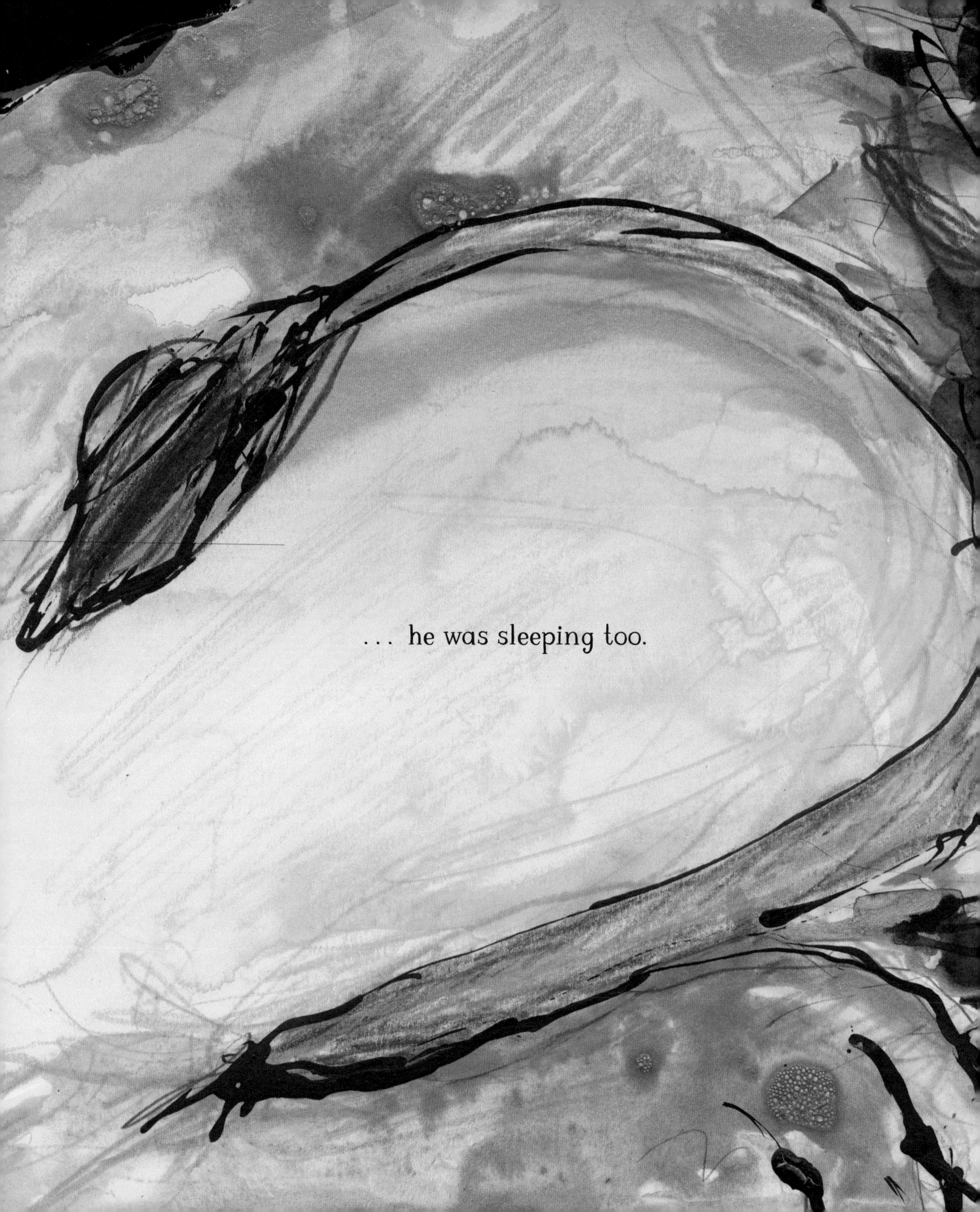

. . . he was sleeping too.

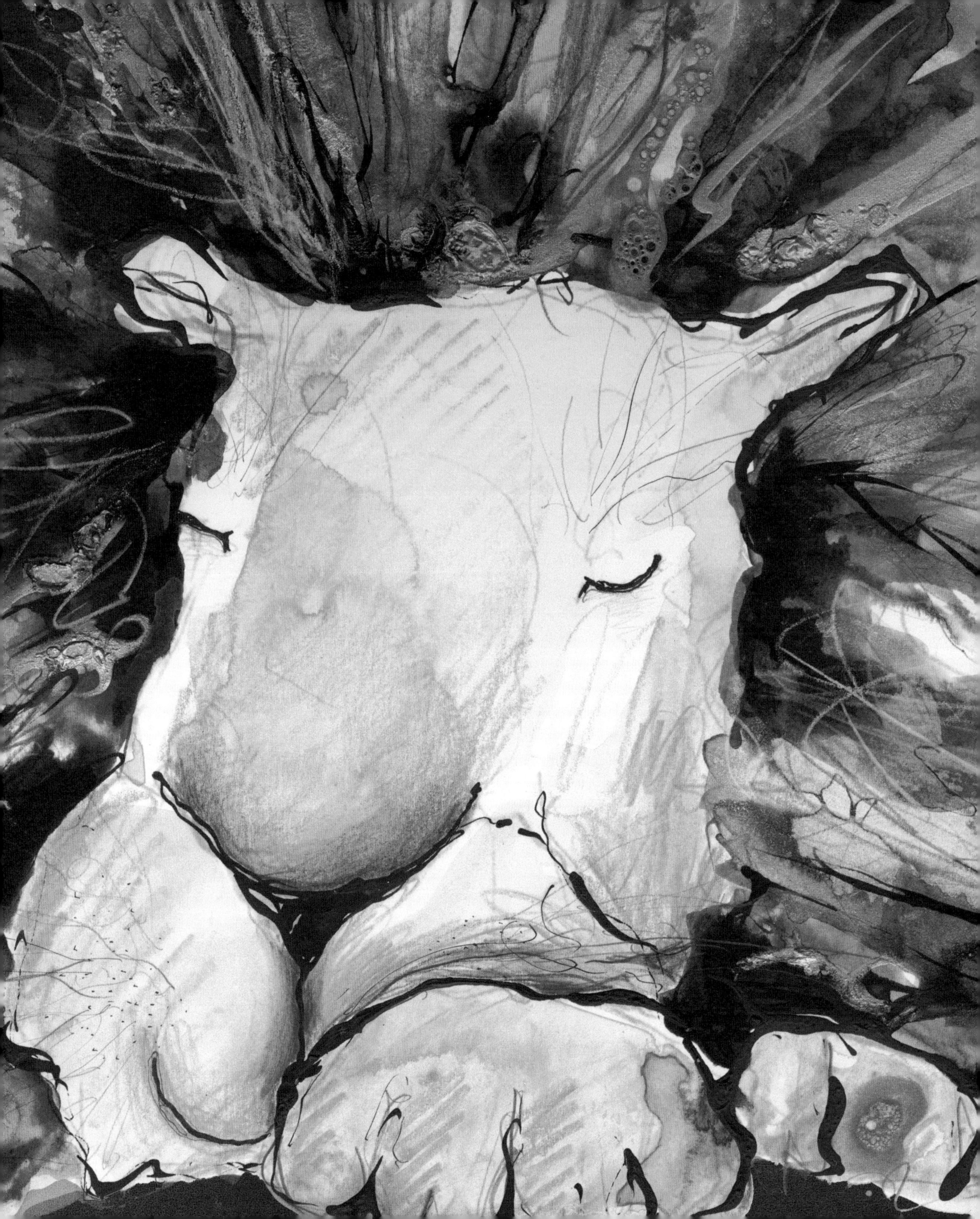

Arlo woke up feeling the sun on his coat.
He had been asleep for hours and felt
happy, fresh and full of energy.

He couldn't wait to tell Owl.

"Little Owl?" roared Arlo. "I slept! Hurray!"
"Well done," came a tired voice from above, "but now you've woken ME up!"

"I'm sorry," said Arlo. "Shall I sing your song to you?" Owl nodded her tired head, and Arlo began to sing.

And while he sang, Owl thought of
the places she would like to go and see.
She imagined flying over open waters,
soaring high and fast, and gliding
through wild forests.

Before she knew it, Owl felt starlight on her feathers.
She had slept through the day, and felt wonderful and rested.

"Hurray!" Owl and Arlo cheered.

"We're pleased YOU'VE slept, but now you've woken us all up," the grumpy lion pride grumbled.
"Sorry," said Arlo.
"But we know what to do," hooted Owl,
and Arlo and Owl sang together . . .

"Have a good stretch from your nose to your toes.
Do a little wriggle, let your eyes gently close.

Relax your whole body, slow your breathing right down,
Imagine you're sinking into the soft ground.

Think about places where you'd like to be,
The things that you'd do there and what you might see.

As you fall into calmness, so comfy and deep,
Your mind will rest and you'll drift off to sleep."

And before long, everyone was asleep, including Arlo.

Everyone, that is, except Owl . . .

. . . who looked out over her friends,
spread her wings and flew
silently away, looking forward
to the long, quiet night ahead.